The Baby Blue Cat and the Dirty Dog Brothers

THE BABY BLUE CAT AND THE DIRTY DOG BROTHERS

Ainslie Pryor

Puffin Books

For Mom

PUFFIN BOOKS
Published by the Penguin Group
Viking Penguin, a division of Penguin Books USA Inc.,
40 West 23rd Street, New York, New York 10010, U.S.A.
Penguin Books Ltd, 27 Wrights Lane, London W8 5TZ, England
Penguin Books Australia Ltd, Ringwood, Victoria, Australia
Penguin Books Canada Ltd, 2801 John Street, Markham, Ontario, Canada L3R 1B4
Penguin Books (N.Z.) Ltd, 182–190 Wairau Road, Auckland 10, New Zealand

Penguin Books Ltd, Registered Offices; Harmondsworth, Middlesex, England

First published in the United States of America by Viking Penguin,
a division of Penguin Books USA Inc., 1987
Published in Picture Puffins 1989
1 3 5 7 9 10 8 6 4 2

LIBRARY OF CONGRESS CATALOGING-IN-PUBLICATION DATA
Pryor, Ainslie.
The baby blue cat and the dirty dog brothers / Ainslie Pryor. p. cm.
Summary: Baby Blue Cat has a romp of a good time playing with the
Dirty Dog Brothers in the sooty ashes and the very big mud puddle.
ISBN 0-14-050769-8
[1. Cleanliness—Fiction. 2. Cats—Fiction. 3. Dogs—Fiction.] I. Title
[PZ7.P9496Baar 1989] [E]—dc 19 89-30226

Printed in Japan by Dai Nippon Printing Co. Ltd.
Set in Avant Garde Book

Have you heard the story of the Baby Blue Cat and the Dirty Dog Brothers?

There was once a Mama Cat
and her four baby cats.

Baby Orange Cat, Baby White Cat,
Baby Striped Cat, and Baby Blue Cat.

Mama Cat loved
all her baby cats
very much.

Mama Cat and her four baby cats
lived next door to the Dogs,
Dad Dog and the Dirty Dog Brothers,
Dwain Dog and Dougie Dog.

Dwain was a yellow dog and
Dougie was a black-and-white dog,

but they were both so dirty
you could hardly tell them apart
except that Dougie had
big floppy ears.

The Dogs and Cats
were good neighbors.

The baby cats usually didn't play with the Dirty Dog Brothers. They preferred to play their own cat games...

except for Baby Blue Cat...

Baby Blue Cat LOVED to play
with the Dirty Dog Brothers.

The best place to play
in the whole neighborhood
was behind the Dogs' house.

Behind the Dogs' house
there was a wonderful dust pit full of
nice sooty ashes and soft grimy dust.

One, two, three, in they would jump!
"Ark bark," said Dwain Dog.
"Wooof booof," said Dougie Dog.
Baby Blue Cat said, "Wow meow!"

Also behind the Dogs' house there was a very nice, very BIG mud puddle. After playing in the dust pit, that's where they'd go.

One, two, three, down they would sit.
"Ark bark."
"Woof booof."
"Wow meow!"

When Baby Blue Cat came home
after a wonderful day of playing
with the Dirty Dog Brothers,

Mama Cat would cover her eyes
with her paws.

"You must be my Baby Blue Cat,"
she sighed. "Let's give you a bath
and find out!"

As Dwain and Dougie stood by,
Mama Cat slipped Baby Blue Cat
into a tub of warm soapy bubbles.

Then with a big soft sea sponge
Mama Cat started,

rub-a-dub-dub, rub-a-dub-dub
from the tops of his ears...

Rub-a-dub-dub, rub-a-dub-dub,
to the tip of his tail.

When she was all done,
rub-a-dub-dub, rub-a-dub-dub,

Mama Cat pulled a baby blue cat
from the bath water.

The Dirty Dog Brothers were amazed.
They went quietly to the tub
and put their paws up on the rim.

They didn't say a word,
but their tails were tick-tocking
back and forth like a clock.

"Would you like a bath too?"
Mama Cat asked.

"Ark bark," said Dwain Dog.
"Wooof booof," said Dougie Dog.
And in they jumped.

The Dirty Dog Brothers
had such fun in the tub.

They played with the soap
and the big soft sea sponge,
and before they knew it...

Rub-a-dub-dub, rub-a-dub-dub,
out of the tub they came,

Dwain, a beautiful yellow dog,
and Dougie, a pretty white dog
with big black spots!

The dogs told Mama Cat
that they had never had
a real bath before.

Then they told her that
they might like to try it again!

Mama Cat told them that
they could come for a bath
as often as they liked.

Then she sent them home
with a whole batch of cookies.

Baby Blue Cat walked them home.

Of course they all went and sat
in the very nice, very BIG mud puddle.

It was the perfect place to eat
a whole batch of cookies.

And now you've heard the story
of the Baby Blue Cat and
the Dirty Dog Brothers.